DECISIONS = DESTINY

ELISSA SCOTT

iUniverse, Inc.
New York Bloomington

DECISIONS = DESTINY

Copyright © 2010 Elissa Scott

All rights reserved. No part of this book may be used or reproduced by any means, graphic, electronic, or mechanical, including photocopying, recording, taping or by any information storage retrieval system without the written permission of the publisher except in the case of brief quotations embodied in critical articles and reviews.

This is a work of fiction. All of the characters, names, incidents, organizations, and dialogue in this novel are either the products of the author's imagination or are used fictitiously.

iUniverse books may be ordered through booksellers or by contacting:

iUniverse
1663 Liberty Drive
Bloomington, IN 47403
www.iuniverse.com
1-800-Authors (1-800-288-4677)

Because of the dynamic nature of the Internet, any Web addresses or links contained in this book may have changed since publication and may no longer be valid. The views expressed in this work are solely those of the author and do not necessarily reflect the views of the publisher, and the publisher hereby disclaims any responsibility for them.

ISBN: 978-1-4502-1838-2 (pbk)
ISBN: 978-1-4502-1839-9 (ebook)

Printed in the United States of America

iUniverse rev. date: 4/27/10

Contents

Chapter 1 = "SO LITTLE GIRL"..1

Chapter 2 = "GRAVESITE TERROR"..5

Chapter 3 = "ACCOMMODATION IN DEATH VALLEY"...11

Chapter 4 = "BREATHING FIRE"..15

Chapter 5 = "THE RUSH OF POWER".....................................19

Chapter 6 = "ICED EYES"..23

Chapter 7 = "AFTER DEATH EXPERIENCES"......................25

Chapter 8 = "BURIED ALIVE"..29

Chapter 9 = "BURNT"..33

Chapter 10 = "ONE-EYED STALKER"....................................37

Chapter 11 = "GOING DOWN"..41

Chapter 12 = "GOING DOWN" - PART 2.................................45

Chapter 13 = "WIRED BLOOD"...49

To my loving family who love me unconditionally

"SO LITTLE GIRL"

"So, little girl, what's your name, mmm? Does your mother know where you are? All alone out here at dusk? Have you noticed no one else is around? Do you know what this means, little girl? My little princess, looks like you're out here all by yourself. So, little one, can I see your pretty young face? Tie that long blonde hair in a ponytail. That'll look real nice to me. Come over here, cross over, just a little—that's all I need—and let me know your name."

Lucy crossed the road and approached the shadow of the man. She noticed his messy hair; his face was dirty and wrinkled. His eyes were glassy and half shut. Lucy felt nervous but couldn't understand why she was moving closer and closer. There seemed to be an energy source that pulled her nearer and nearer. Suddenly she could smell him. He didn't smell nice. The man looked down at her. He looked mean but his voice was inviting.

Lucy's heart began to beat faster. She wanted to run away but her feet were stuck solid to the ground. She asked him nervously, "What's your name?"

He looked back at her. "Little girl, why do you want to know?"

"Um." She hesitated and took a quick breath. "I'm not sure. I don't know why," she nervously replied. The man's face started to twitch and change as the sun began to set behind the hills.

Goose bumps formed on her arms, across the back of her neck, and on her bare legs below the hem of her school uniform.

Lucy stared, mesmerized. He leaned forward and touched her softly on the arm, giving it a little squeeze as he let go. She looked down at his hands and noticed some of his fingers were missing. One finger on the right hand was very short; fingers on the left hand were stumps or missing. Any remaining fingernails were broken, filthy, and black. *Where does he live?* she wondered. *Why's he so dirty?*

Lucy often played outside after school but had never seen him before. She remembered her mother making breakfast. "Remember, Lucy, don't cross the road and don't speak to strangers," her mother said every day before Lucy left for school, today being no exception. Lucy thought about running back to her mother but her body and mind were frozen in place. *Why can't I move?* she thought in a panic after fruitlessly testing one foot.

Blinking suddenly, Lucy found herself focusing on the stranger's distorted face. It looked different. It had changed once again. She took one step closer and noticed movement in his eye. *Is that a leech?* She focused harder. "*Gross*!" She didn't remember seeing anything similar in her nature textbooks.

This thing had started to crawl along the stranger's left lower eyelid, sucking the moisture out of the eye as it crept along. The creature's body was now moist and slippery. Its black belly seemed to be getting fatter and fuller with the liquid that it had just consumed. The stranger's eye had begun to close and sink into itself. He looked sickly pale, and his skin took on a yellow tinge.

"Hey, are you okay?" she yelled at him. "Hurry up and get that thing out of your eye! Hurry, mister! It's yucky."

He squinted and foamed at the mouth. "I can't, little girl. It's too late," he slurred. "The creature has sucked all the goodness out of me and all that's left is evil and nasty."

So run now, little girl. Run! Leave me! Go quickly before it's too late!" He screamed. "You've got two minutes! You must go before its way too late!"

Lucy spun around and bolted towards home. She got to the edge of the road which was now busy with evening traffic. She started to whimper when she realized she couldn't cross. She felt her energy draining.

I shouldn't have crossed the road in the first place! she scolded herself. She could see her mother on the phone in the kitchen from where she was standing. *She's probably calling friends to find me!* she thought as she tried to lift a hand to wave. But before her hand reached her waist she heard footsteps coming up behind her. Her spine stiffened when she realized it was too late. She let out a desperate scream as she felt both mutilated hands grab her shoulders.

Ends

"GRAVESITE TERROR"

"Cathy, I'm so sorry. Joseph's gone."

"No!"

"Oh Cathy, yes it's true." A black hearse hit Joseph and knocked him to the ground, killing him instantly. Apparently the rusted out motor underneath caught his denim jacket, carrying him an extra 50 metres over the hot asphalt, broken bottles, and garbage left on the road after the council clean up.

"Oh my God!"

Tears start to pour down Mum's face.

"No! No!"

Mum let out a loud wail, slammed down the receiver, and fell to the floor. After rocking side to side she turned onto her right side and curled into a fetal position. She froze in place.

My brother was buried after a private memorial for family and close friends only. Our lives changed forever.

"Mum, your friends are worried," I told her a month later. "You've been isolating yourself. You haven't put any makeup on and you don't look well. And I don't know why you don't want *me* going out. Please, Mum, I want to see my friends."

"Sorry, love, but you're all I've got left."

"Mum, will you speak to your counsellor?"

"I will."

She kept her word. And the result was a move to another neighborhood that didn't hold all of our family memories. We moved during Easter week.

I was surprised that my mum gave me permission to ride my bike to the gravesite to let Joseph know we moved.

When I arrived at cemetery I noticed a skinny man riding a mower. He was staring at me, and as he got closer I saw that his eyes weren't the same size. He raised his hand and motioned for me to leave.

"Get off the grass, little girl. You're in my way."

He picked up garden scissors and waved me away again.

"Get a move on now. You hear me, don't you, little girl?"

I steered towards the road but in my haste I lost my sense of direction and couldn't find Joseph's grave. I stopped and balanced myself and the bike on one foot. I heard an engine behind me. When I looked over my shoulder I saw a black hearse heading straight for me, and fast.

When he got closer I could see that he was the man who was just mowing. His hands appeared to be shaking vigorously on the steering wheel. He was bent forward as though he expected his body weight to help the vehicle go faster. Those eyes gave me chills. He stopped abruptly, and the tires threw pebbles into my skin.

"Hey! What are you doing?" I yelled at him. When I backed up, I fell onto the grass. My head barely missed the concrete curb.

"Are you crazy?" I yelled again. My heart was beating so hard my chest hurt.

He rolled down the window until he could lean out.

"I'm coming to get you. You need to be taught a lesson, little girl. You should do what you're told."

With that comment the reverse lights flicked back on and the car still idled motionless. The exhaust pipe began to rev up, blowing out blue and black smoke. A massive bang came out of the car; it skidded back to where I was standing.

"What are you doing?" I screamed at the top of my lungs.

"You can't see into my car, little girl. My windows are as black as my soul."

"But I can see you!" I yelled with false bravado. "You don't scare me!"

I disentangled myself from my bike and bolted towards him. He didn't flinch. I peered into the back of the hearse, and when my eyes returned to the driver, he had disappeared.

"Where are you?"

When he reappeared, he was standing next to the hearse, holding the passenger door open. I noticed that one eye looked like it was half shut.

He mouthed, "Get in, little girl."

"No! You're crazy!"

"Did you not hear me, little girl? Get in *now*! The longer I wait for you the harder it's going to be when I finally get you. You will have wished you had never disobeyed me in the first place."

I tried to keep my legs from trembling but I was sure he noticed that I was frozen stiff. With my peripheral vision I tried to find an escape path, but I saw his arm reaching for me across the front hood.

"Leave me alone!" I screamed, wondering if anyone would hear me.

He clawed at the air again. I leaned backwards, out of his reach. He was foaming at the mouth and I could smell his rotten breath.

"Come here right now and do as you are told … or else."

The pupil in his normal eye dilated as he tried to grab me again. He pulled his arm back and growled in frustration.

"Girl, listen here. This is your last warning, so get in and do as you are told. I'm going to hurt you. You understand? You'll regret your actions."

My right foot was numb, and I knew I couldn't get away on my bike; he'd have enough time to stop me. I half-ran and half-limped away as fast as I could.

The crazy man revved the engine and started coming after me. My heart was pounding, and breathing was hard.

He caught up. "Where do you think you're going, little girl? There's no place to hide. You will never discover the secrets of this cemetery. You will never know who I really am, I have this place covered. I will get you sooner than later, and you will be mine forever."

He came after me on foot. I tried to run faster. The bundles of flowers I passed were just blurs of color. "Ow!" I screamed aloud. Something cut my leg, and it felt like it was still there. I looked down and saw a thorn embedded in my shin, and a heavy stream of blood flowing steady, already staining the top of my sock.

"I can smell your blood, girly."

"Why are you so interested in getting me?" I yelled while still running. "Why are you so evil?"

I was drenched with sweat, and my sock was stained a bright red. I wondered if he was really the groundkeeper of this cemetery or just a crazy man who hung out here.

I lay down next to Joseph's plaque, trying to catch my breath, but I knew I couldn't rest for long.

"Where are you, little girl? I know you're near. I can smell your blood. I bet you got caught on Mrs. Jackson's roses. I have a piece of your shirt too. Mmmm … Lovely. I'm going to get you. It's only a matter of time, girly."

I looked at my shirt and saw that the hem was ripped. I hadn't noticed. But he did. I was leaving clues. And then he went silent.

"You'll never know what's below the surface," he rambled on. "I'll make sure of that for now and forever."

I stayed low to the ground behind a thick, old tree. I could hear leaves crackling. Footsteps. It sounded like more than one person. They were coming closer.

"Lucy, what are you doing?"

"Mum?" I looked up. She was standing next to the man.

"Mum!" I screamed. "Get away from him! Get away now! He's crazy."

"He's only showing me to Joseph's gravesite. I'm lost."

"No! Mum …" I took in another lunch of air. "No!"

She bent down to look closer.

"Lucy, what happened to your leg?"

"We have to get away from that man!" I screamed into Mum's concerned face. "He's crazy! He's after me!"

Mum stood up and reached down towards me.

"Take my hand, Lucy. Let's go get your bike."

She didn't believe me. I let her help me up and we walked off together. Her hand was trembling. *Maybe she does believe me*, I thought to myself.

I looked back over her shoulder to where the caretaker was still standing.

He smirked at me. "Next time," he mouthed.

Ends

"ACCOMMODATION IN DEATH VALLEY"

"Lucy, do you believe in the steps you will need to climb up into my heart? Why are you investing your time to find out where I am? You crashed. Ouch. Why is everyone freaking out? Lucy, where are you?"

"The mechanics and fears that are in your mind are the reasons why you can't move forward."

"The power of moving forward isn't that hard. Why does that keep you from finding the focus you will need to let me be your dominator? Avoid me? No, Lucy, you know that we both have the answers. Seriously, it's a great idea. It's holiday time, a good time to visit your family at the farm house. What could be better? We'll be out of town together. Nice all round, really!"

"Pack up your little things, Lucy. We're leaving within the hour."

"Mum, do you remember how to get there?"

"Yes, love. If we want to reach the town by noon we'll have to get moving pretty soon."

"Are we taking the Volkswagen this time? We may as well as we're only going for the weekend."

Mum doesn't know that there's someone else going in our car. I tried to tell her but she didn't believe me.

We drove down the freeway and turned left, through the valley, and up over the hill. The farm—our holiday home—was as we left it last time.

The seasons had changed, though, since we were here last. The town festival was booked for this weekend, so the town will be buzzing.

We unpacked and were hungry. Mum had gone out back to pick some rocket for our salad. She was breathing heavily when she returned.

"Lucy, look out the window. Do you see anyone near the shed?"

"No. But can you hear someone calling my name?"

"No, Lucy, you're imagining it. It's just windy and it's the whistling through the trees that you can hear."

His hunger was intensifying and his energy was pulling me outside. I could feel it throughout my body as I walked out onto the veranda and looked towards the shed.

On the right hand side of the shed was the shadow of a man. My arms were covered in goose pimples.

Why is this happening to me? Why is this parasite following me?

It's inevitable we go off track; his reasons and habits follow me, trying to influence my thoughts.

Is this finally the end? When will this voice disappear?

"Mum, I need you!" I yelled. "Can you see the man behind the shed?"

Mum peeked out.

"Lucy, what's wrong with you? You told me no one was there. Why do you carry on like this? It's the wind from that direction, that's all. I hear nothing and see nothing. Come back in for lunch."

As I sat at the kitchen table I saw him peering at me through the kitchen window.

"Mum, look! There he is. He's hungry. Can we feed him?"

"Feed who? There's no one there."

"Mum, his stomach area is enormous."

"Lucy, you've got to stop having these thoughts. This fantasy isn't healthy for you or our family. You're so passionate for this friend of yours to be real. The description of your fantasy friend isn't normal. Young girls talk nice to their make believe best friends. Lucy, I'm at my wit's end. What am I going to do with you? You drain me, and its taking its toll. It's been 24 hours now. It's time to stop. The doctor told you to live in the present."

No one believes me.

I went out. The wind picked up suddenly. Leaves crunched under my feet. "Help," I called out. "Help." No one came. *Is this really going to be the end of my life? I wondered.*

I felt something under my foot.

"Are those bones? Why are there bones around here? Man, whose bones are these? What have you done? Man this isn't good. Not good at all. Can you hear me?" Lucy whimpered.

"Where are you, girl?"

"I'm over here. What do you want? What have you done? Whose bones are these?"

"Girl, these are the skeletons of death. You need not worry your pretty head. At the end you'll find out, it's only your minds deadly valley of despair."

*End*s

"BREATHING FIRE"

"Welcome, everyone!" the bus driver yelled out of the open door. "All aboard! The wilderness tour is about to begin."

I placed my blue backpack next to the other bags that were already stacked up underneath the bus and held onto mum's hand as we boarded. A yellow tag with the scribbled name of "Roy Jones" was half-hanging over the seat in front of me. Roy had obviously been on the bus to put his carry-ons in the overhead locker.

Mum and I sat down next to each other as a blonde, stocky man wearing knee-length shorts over smooth-shaven legs boarded. He looked young and spoke to the driver with an accent.

Mum said, "He sounds Scandinavian."

"Bet he's Norwegian," I told her. "I think he has blue eyes." I tried not to stare as I examined him via my peripheral vision. "Well, at least *one* blue eye cause I can't see into the squinty one," I whispered.

"I think Roy Jones is a wildlife photographer," mum whispered back. "I remember reading that he was wounded by an animal that snuck up on him. Maybe that's what happened."

A crackling noise came through the intercom. Our fat-bellied bus driver stood up and leaned back on the steering wheel. "Good day, everyone!" he said loudly. "Welcome! For some of you, it's your first time, and for others it's a repeated tour. We're going to do things differently this time. You will be asked individually to introduce yourselves to the other passengers, talk about your strengths, weaknesses and personal goals for this trip.

You'll then take a seat next to someone you don't know," he finished with a smirk and an arching eyebrow that sent forth a challenge.

"Are you going to be okay without me?" mum asked.

I rolled my eyes. "Of course, mum."

"Just remember to have your asthma inhaler when you move seats."

"So, bus load, who wants to go first?" the driver asked cheerily.

I put my hand straight up and into the air. Everyone's eyes turned and moved towards my direction.

"My name's Lucy. I'm 10 years old and from Australia. I love my long black curly hair. I have green eyes, wear size 4 shoes, have my ears pierced like my mum, and suffer badly from asthma. My mum is my strength; I love her heaps. Wave mum!"

Mum gave a quick wave towards the front and back.

"I don't breathe properly," I continued, "and I need to take drugs to stay alive. These drugs make me lose weight, and I don't have a lot of energy. I get panic attacks, and I grow slower compared to other kids. We came on the tour to see whether the wilderness air would strengthen my lungs."

When I started to wheeze the bus driver interrupted. "Thank you, Lucy. That was great! I'll place you next to that fellow with blonde hair." He pointed at Roy Jones.

Wow, I thought to myself. *"How lucky am I?"*

Overly excited, I forgot to take a breath and caught my trousers on the edge of the seat as I headed for the aisle. I heard a whisper.

"Lucy, did you remember to bring your inhaler?"

I looked back at mum. She mouthed, "It's in your back pocket."

Roy looked calm and relaxed. I was mesmerized by his eyes, and I melted at the sight of his brown muscular arms. I slipped down into my new seat.

Roy took the microphone and introduced himself as a photographer for Worldwide Wilderness.

"I'm 28 years old, Capricorn—if anybody cares," he added with a short laugh, "and from Norway."

I looked back at mum with an "I told you so" glare.

"I spend nine months of the year living in the wilderness waiting for those special moments when I can capture amazing pictures of creatures big or small." His grin got bigger. "Translated, this means I'm single."

He paused for the anticipated laughter.

"I want everyone to learn about nature and its beauty. I'm very patient and compassionate. I get annoyed with lazy, uncaring humans who don't respect the environment. My goal is to be the best in my field and to raise funds for Planet Ark."

I looked around. Everyone seemed inspired, and his accent kept the captives captivated. I noticed that my mum was in a trance. Her glasses had fogged up.

"Right, everyone," the bus driver bellowed. "Time to get this bus on the tracks."

The tour guide took her seat, the driver put the bus in drive, the engine backfired three times, and we were off. Tiny drops of moisture appeared on the window ledge as we headed away. I chewed on my last long fingernail as I looked out the window.

A few minutes into the drive there was a deafening explosion that jerked me forward. I presumed the engine had backfired again but when I turned to find mum she was gone.

And so was everyone behind me. The bus was engulfed in flames. I heard the indescribable screams of people burning to death.

I felt my heart began to race and my breathing was erratic. Roy looked at me with an intensified one-eye stare. We were frozen in time, shocked, shaking, and gasping for air. I reached into my back pocket but my inhaler was gone.

Roy launched from his seat and up to the front. The bus driver was pressed against the steering wheel, his fists melted into the hard plastic. His smoldering arms slid onto his belly as he past away.

Roy's voice was scratchy from the smoke he yelled out, "Is there anyone here who can help me get her?" No voices returned. Only the sounds of crackling fire and erratic gasps could be heard as I struggled to fill my lungs; whimpering my last breath, slurring, "mum, *pleaseee* don't leave me alone with him."

Ends

"THE RUSH OF POWER"

Lightning from the stranger's body cut deep into Lucy, excited by its impending journey. It began at the top with short bursts of electric pulses that flowed from left to right, jolting and rocking the 15-year-old's world. Lucy rocked from side to side. *When will this stop? What if it never does?*

"Lucy, little girl, can you hear me? Lucy, you must understand, you are mine. Why fight this motion? Let it drift over time. I hear you breathe. Why so slowly? Little girl, the torture of it must go on, hour by hour, minute by minute. I know it's exhausting—its power so repulsive—but you are mine. You hear me? Mine forever."

"I will fight you!" Lucy squealed. "I will cross the highs and lows of time. You must know, surely, that you can't control me. Stranger, stop searching. Listen and feel it. You can't take control of my brain. I know you will try as you cut inside and seep into my flesh, but you are only allowed to move from left to right. You think that this is a long journey; maybe it will be, maybe it won't be, and maybe it will be longer than you think."

"Lucy, we must continue this torture; it's good for you."

"Stranger, I can't breathe. Stranger, can you hear me? You're hurting me. Let me go! Just remember, Stranger, I will win, and you will lose and eventually get caught. Someone will come for me. Someone will notice I'm missing."

"No, they won't. You have it all wrong, Lucy. I warned you that I was evil. "Judging from the way you appear now, you didn't listen. So now it's your turn to suffer, and suffer you will."

"Stranger, are you still here? I can feel you, but I can't touch you. You travel downwards day and night; every waking moment you seek and search, waiting to be found. Is it just in my mind? My head hurts from the uncertainty of not knowing where you've gone. Come back, Stranger. I see specks of dust floating by. Is that you? Do you breathe like me or do you breathe only when the wind blows? Why don't you answer me? I can't hear you anymore. Speak up. Can you hear me? Come back!"

"Why is this time so short, Lucy? Tick tock. Those seconds, girlie, were just lost in time. I'm over here; just seek and you will find."

"Hello, Stranger. Are you in there? Please answer me. I'm feeling nervous and anxious and can't wait to see you again. My eyes roll from left to right and I need to sneeze. You are around me; I can feel you and smell you. Stranger, you smell rotten. I know my mum wants to keep me safe. I feel safe when I feel her sunshine around me. Soon mum will wonder where I am. It's getting dark and I'm still across the road. Mum will start to worry; it's only a matter of time."

Hey, Stranger, there's no belting rain. Why did the Earth take our power and raise it back up and into your half-shut eye? Or was the world globe your one *big* eye?

"Help me. Can anyone hear me? Someone, please answer me. Don't leave me out here all alone."

"I'm passing our church on the side of the road. The beautiful ladies are singing out loud. Can you hear them? Can you hear their lovely voices? They each send a message of love across the land for you.

"The land is so dry. Why is this so?" The hands of these ladies are cracked and tunneled dry. No moisture for anyone. No tears from above or strikes of thunder as you roar? Are you so unhappy with us all?

"Why did you disappear?" Only the shadows across the way give me hope that you'll be back here one day. I wait and wonder. Night closes in and day breaks; still no sign that you are coming back.

"Why do I have to wait this long? Where have you gone?" Some of us get taken at birth; others depart as teenagers. Why is it that the rest of us wait a lifetime? How do you choose whose next? I sit still and wonder. Why does life end so quickly for some and so painfully for others? What is your story? What is your pain? Do you punish us one by one because we're so bad? How do you see through that one strange eye?

"Do you point with the pupil of your working eye? Do you a keep scorecard and mark off when we are good, bad, and truly evil? Why don't you answer me, Stranger? Stranger, where have you gone?"

"What was that? I think I just saw you. Did you ripple and float by? Over there in that muddy water, is that you? No, of course not; it's not you. I must be mistaken; it wasn't you. Silly me. What was I thinking? I imagined that I just saw you. But I do wonder where you've gone. Maybe I did see you. Oh yes, I know who you are. You're my reflection. Yes, that's the answer to it all!"

You reflect, day in and day out, as we walk together. Yes, I see you now. You're my shadow, my footprint, my mind, and even my breath. How silly I was to not realize that you were frozen in my mind.

Ends

"ICED EYES"

I hate my life so much that ending it seems the only way out.

Can you imagine that one human can be so nasty with the words they say?

Can you imagine that one human can be so manipulative?

Can you imagine that one human can poison one small mind?

Can hate control one's desire?

H is for Hurry. *A* is for Anger. *T* is for Terrorising. *E* is for Execution.

I hate him …

He follows me around day and night. I can't escape. Do I give into him? Do I surrender? I'm so confused. What do I do? What is the cost of freedom? When will I be free? Totally free? Free from this hell?

He comes into my mind; left brain senses his arrival. His eyes pierce me as he focuses on me and looks me over, up and down. His eyes flicker with glee.

Why can't anybody else see him?

Mum doesn't understand. I've tried to show her what I see. Am I the only one who sees the world like this?

He is so cruel, tempting me into his world that I can't leave on my own. It's so captivating. When will I be free?

This man has no conscience; he doesn't care. He says he does, but it's all been lies. I see the truth that lies under those wicked eyes. His eyes lead me down into his polluted soul.

He wants me to fester and become infected. Like him. I am his obsession.

Why am I his chosen one? I'm tired of trying to work it out. It's been so long. I am exhausted. I want the pain to stop.

"Lucy? Lucy? Where are you?"

"Go away, man. Leave me alone."

"No, Lucy. Come here, little one."

"Go away! I hate you! Don't you understand? Leave me alone!"

"No! Stop that, Lucy, you naughty little girl. You know that this is right; it's been proven day and night. You must come, cross over and be by my side. I want you, now and forever. You are mine!"

"Never! I'll make sure that you never succeed!"

"Calm down, my sweet girl. Now I can see into your beautiful eyes, my love. You don't *really* hate me. You may *dislike* me, but hate is such a strong word."

"I *do* hate you! Go away! Leave me alone!"

"I can't, Lucy. You are the chosen one—the chosen one for me."

Ends

"AFTER DEATH EXPERIENCES"

"Lucy, do you ever take the time to look at the stars and wonder what's out there? Trillions of stars burning brightly in the quiet night sky. Do you watch how they sparkle and glisten? If you look hard enough they can even fall before your eyes, playing little tricks with your mind. See that star cluster over there? Those are your stars, Lucy. That's your birth star. August 13 is your birthday. You're a Leo—a lion."

"What are you, Mum?"

"April is Aries—the ram."

"See up there?"

Our heads turned in unison.

"In those stars over there is a horn shape. That's my star."

"So I'm a lion and you're a sheep?"

"Yes," Mum answered, laughing.

"Cool, I get it. I can see that shape so clearly now that you point it out. Shit! What was that? Did you see that, Mum?"

"Yeah. I think I did."

"Did you see the explosion at the top of the ram's horn? Mum? What's happening? Watch out!"

"No, Lucy. Leave me."

"Why are you burning? I'll get the hose!"

"No! Leave me. This is a sign from God. He wants me in his promised land. It's my time."

"That's stupid! It's only your hair that's burning. Have you gone crazy? Why are my legs growing fur?" Lucy asked after glancing down. "My knee hurts. My bones and muscles! Ouch. What's the universe doing to us?"

"I don't know, dear. My head really hurts where the bones are popping out."

"They're horns, Mum! Your ears have been burnt off and you're not crying? Don't you feel the pain?"

"Lucy, do you believe in God?"

"Mum, this isn't the time …"

"If you believe in God, you feel no pain at death. You too, my love, have changed. The new hair you have all over you is magnificent—a lovely tinge of orange and yellow covering strong muscles. You're a real lion now."

"Lucy, I think we are the chosen ones. We must respect our new roles with pride. Our lives have changed forever. We are dead and no longer exist. The transition phase between life and death is quick."

"It's true, everyone sees the light in this phase; so real, yes it's us, we are the first phase of recreation. We are reincarnated into our birth signs, I'm the Aries ram and you are the Leo lion. How lucky do you feel that we now know the answers to the after death experience?"

"Mum? Where's everyone else?"

"It's those who believe and go to pray that get to cross straight over into their respective birth signs and go on forever. Those who are born in June, for example, become little crabs in the ocean. Those who sort of believe and don't go to church get stuck in the first phase forever."

"What's going to happen to us?"

"We must not be seen by the leftover humans. We must hide. But, Lucy, where can we hide? Soon it will be morning and your father will be looking for us. I feel part of this internal transition is for us to be constantly on the move. We must protect the good people of the planet and wait. We must not be seen. If someone notices us we will be lowered down underneath as experiments. We must keep this after-death experience our secret. We must go now."

"But, Mum, your whole body hasn't fully changed."

"I know; it's only my head that changed. Aries is ruled by the head. We must try and find others like us. It's important for our survival to get to the other side. We'll find more power if we join forces with the other star signs. Our timeframe is thirty days because the sun then moves into the next zodiac sign. We must be ready to be reincarnated into our whole self."

"Mum, I'm worried. Will I end up South Africa and you be sent to New Zealand? Will being apart offer us fulfillment and happiness?"

"Only our quiet minds will remember each other," Mum said with a sad smile. "I will miss you, but understand this is our new journey of time." Mum suddenly looked alarmed. "Duck down. Hurry! Someone's coming."

It was our neighbor, Brian. "Hello, Aries and Leo. It's me, Sagittarius," he said, waving.

"Look, Lucy. He's half man, half horse. Brian once told me that he didn't pray for three days in a row last year, so look what's happened. He hasn't made it fully over to the other side. He's stuck. Brian, have you see anyone else?"

"No, I haven't."

"Together must continue our search. We need to cover as much ground as we can. We need a lot of power to be completely transformed. The Virgo sign is the Dr Jekyll-Mr Hyde type who will try to pierce our soft skin and sap up our energy. We must stay away from them," Mum cautioned.

I wondered how she knew so much more than me.

"Virgos must not get on the path," Mum went on. "Their breeding on Earth isn't yet complete. We must reject them. All of them. They must stay."

"Watch out!"

We turned towards a massive fireball tube as it rolled towards us. Its aim was to hit us in order to strike out our tunnel. Somehow I knew that the explosion was meant to help us; it would create a path to let us cross over to the other side. I was excited about seeing old family members; but knew it wouldn't be long before we would be taken back to Earth as newborns.

Ends

"BURIED ALIVE"

Have you ever thought about death? Was it during your teenage years with all its inherent drama? When you married or had your first child? Or when your grandmother was dying of cancer, living out the last days of her shortened life? It's only human for the living to think about dying. In my case, it began last summer.

I thought about death during my teen years, which were mostly spent at school. From 18-30 I raised my child and stepchildren. I remember summers at the beach and dark winter nights under our quilts, in front of a roaring fire. I remember their laughter, but now it fades away and out of my mind.

Lucy, time to make myself another cup of tea, I prodded myself. I watched the old kettle and listened to the old wall clock in the hall. I listened to the soft strokes of time and wondered about the last twenty years of my life. Where has all this time gone? *Tick/tock.* What will happen to my frail old body now?

The local postman skidded into my driveway and crossed the front lawn, leaving his daily tire mark in the same worn out grooves of dirt. It's morning. The neighbor's dog continuously barks—a daily routine—but the noise fades as the postman leaves.

I look out and see a pink envelope sticking out of my letterbox. Opening the seal, I find a pretty flyer—an advertisement for the local funeral parlor. *How did they know I had cancer? Which doctor's database did this company buy? Does everyone know that I'm going to die?* I wondered as I slowly climbed the stairs.

I decided I would call them, but as I reached the top step my ankle twisted and I fell, hitting my head on the banister. "Oh it hurts," I groaned. Everything's blurry and I'm having trouble breathing. *Will someone ever come? Did someone see me fall?*

I lay there, waiting, until it became cooler and the shadows disappeared.

No one came. *Does anyone care? Why am I alone? Where is everyone?* I was disoriented. I must have passed out cold.

I heard the Kookaburras and knew it was another morning. The milkman arrived.

"Ms Lucy? Everything okay?"

I couldn't reply. My tongue was dry and swollen. I presumed my mouth was open all night. I could hear an ambulance siren. It was coming closer. It was coming for me.

I felt myself being lifted up, but not into an ambulance. It was a hearse. I heard someone say "funeral." The driver turned. It was him. He just shook his head with sorrow. His eyes were still the same. He snarled at me.

I reached for his mutilated hand but couldn't find it in the dark. *I love you, sir. Is that what you want to hear? It's never too late. I really love you.*

I heard him tell the milkman that I was finally dead. How could anyone let him anywhere near me? *I can't be dead. I can hear. Someone has to know!*

Again, I tried in vain to reach out.

Please don't be sad. It's not the end. I'm still here. I can see you from inside this box. Please, sir, don't close the lid. Why can't you see that I'm alive? Please don't leave me. I don't want to be buried alive!

Ends

"BURNT"

"I'm so sorry, Roy. There's nothing that anyone can do now. I can't express how sorry we are. Our hospital and staff are horrified that this happened. This should never have happened to you. Take a minute to steady yourself. I'm going to get the file from the medical records. I want to make sure that I explain everything to you in detail."

Lucy left the room, and Roy was now alone.

Take a minute? Not likely. Someone will pay for this! Someone will have to take responsibility. How am I ever going to function from now on? What will my life be like back home at Norah Head? Will I embarrass myself? What happened to the hospital staff on duty that day? Why wasn't the doctor in charge looking after my operation? Who really did the cutting?

The door opened. The curtain swung around and Lucy reappeared, carrying the black folder. She glanced at the first page.

"Okay if I sit at the edge of the bed?" she asked.

"Suppose so."

Lucy looked down at the folder. Her hands shook as she turned the page. "I'm going to be completely honest with you. This is the incident report dated December 19, 2006, 3:13 pm. Operation theatre room 62. Present and in attendance: two nurses, one intern, and one doctor in charge.

"Lucy?" Roy interrupted. "Am I going to be okay?"

"Let me read on, Roy. It's important that I finish."

He nodded.

"At 4:06 pm the cautery—that's the heating element—is turned on and your anesthetic was administered. Dr. Andrews made the incision to expose the bowel and inspected the area of suspected cancer. Both nurses check the monitors and confirm each other's readings. At that point, everything is fine. The intern is noted as being present as an observer only."

She paused and looked at him. "Roy, do you remember at the beginning of your operation, Dr. Andrews let you know that they would be cutting the cancer-affected area out of the bowel?"

Roy nodded.

"It says that, once they got inside, it didn't look as bad, so they decided to just burn off the cancer cells. They all thought it would be a better option for you—quicker recovery and early departure from the hospital. You agreed earlier, on the consent form, that you'd be okay if the scope of the operation changed once they opened you up." She held up the page so he could see it.

He nodded again.

"The handwriting is messier on the next page, but I'll try to figure it out," she continued. "Looks like the intern was to let the doctor and one nurse know when the cautery timer went off. The doctor popped out to the bathroom, the timer went off, and instead of letting the doctor know when he re-entered the room, and the intern decided that another twenty seconds would completely burn all the affected areas. In fact, that's when the damage to the lining of your bowel occurred. I'm so sorry, Roy. If the cautery was switched off when the timer had buzzed your bowel would have been fine.

The final page says you've been so badly burned that the scar tissue won't ever heal.

The hole in the lining of your bowel is causing the leaking . . ."

Roy jolted and threw his arms around himself. Lucy fell onto the vinyl floor. When she looked at Roy, his face was red, he was shaking with rage and his left eye was seeping. He reached towards Lucy and grabbed her by the neck.

"Where's that intern now?" he leaned forward and screamed.

"I don't know," she whispered as he loosened his grip. "Please calm down; the patients can hear you."

"I don't care, girl! You will pay for this!"

"Let me go," she pleaded, wondering why someone hadn't already called security.

"Calm down?" he growled into her face. "Does anyone know if my cancer is gone? Does *anyone* know? I came in for an operation for cancer and now I need nappies! This is unforgivable. I'll get you back for this!" He pulled Lucy's hair and moved his face less than an inch from hers. "How does a leaky bowel get fixed, girl?" he screamed at her, propelling spit onto her skin. "Are you going to be with me 'round the clock' to change my nappies? What will my life be like outside this hellhole? Do you even care, girl? Who's going to help me?" He dribbled the last words as he fell back, exhausted, onto the pillow.

Lucy bolted to the door, fighting the desire to stay and console him. She needed to alert the staff.

Ends

"ONE-EYED STALKER"

"Sorry about the night shift, love. I'll be at the reception area in the main lobby in case you have to find me."

"I'm leaving now. If you want, you can heat up the leftovers in the fridge and I'll catch you in the morning before you head off to work."

"Bye," said Lucy and planted a kiss on his bald head.

I hope tonight's shift will be relatively easy, Lucy thought as she looked for her knitting bag. *Should be with the day patients released.*

As she parked, she noticed the surveillance cameras had been reinstalled and a lone security guard walking up and down the rows. She tensed a bit when she heard the guard's voice but soon realized he was talking into his Bluetooth earpiece.

Walking into work she caught her reflection in the glass entry doors. The hydrogen street lights reflected back onto the glass. She'd gotten used to them. She was no longer spooked by the weird shapes and shadows the lights made in the grass.

Lucy pressed the elevator button; wondering if had been fixed when it didn't appear after a minute. *How many calls does it take to maintenance to get this done?* When it finally arrived, a man with two young boys exited. He looked at Lucy apologetically. *The little buggers apparently hit the button for every floor*, she realized.

She was alone for the ride up to the main level. When the doors opened, she looked to her left and right—a regular routine—before exiting. The aroma of flowers greeted Lucy as she entered the lobby.

She took out her knitting project—a cap for Keith's bald head—before settling into her seat. No worries now. It would be ready in time for their twentieth wedding anniversary.

Lucy jolted when she caught a shadow out of the corner of her eye. Her heart raced and her sweaty hands dropped a knitting needle. She took her time retrieving the needle, too nervous to look up, but the needle wasn't there. On the way up, she bumped her head on the table.

She sensed someone was there, watching her. She could hear breathing. *A patient?* she wondered as she looked over the desk.

A second passes and another shadow crosses the vinyl floor. Her heart beats faster. Keeping her eyes lowered, she was too nervous to look up; the man's breath was closing in on her.

This man was bent over and leaning forward, staring. His eye socket was seeping fluid, one hand was holding his IV lines, which he had apparently disengaged from their poles and the other hand was holding the end of a tube that seemed to originate from his abdomen.

"Can I help you?" Lucy asked, trying to sound friendly rather than nervous. "Did you come down from level five?" She remembered reading an internal e-mail that warned the nurses about a problem patient. It described him as needing a feeding tube.

"Are you looking for this?" the one-eyed patient asked, in a sedated whisper. He leaned further forward with the needle, but not far enough.

Lucy presumed his range of motion was limited. "Yes, thank you," she said. "I'll come around. If you have surgical stitches, I don't want you tearing them. So off you go now you need to get back to your bed."

The man staggered, tripping over his wires. Lucy tried to steady him but he fell sideways. He stabbed her in the neck as they both tried to stop his fall. The one-eyed man grunted on impact, got up quickly despite the entangled tubes and fled when he saw Lucy collapsed on the floor, blood pouring from her neck and pooling on the vinyl tile.

Night became day, Lucy's body lay motionless, after all these years the one-eyed stalker thought he had finally won.

Ends

"GOING DOWN"

"Keith, love, I need to pop into town. Do you want to join me?"

"No, I'm just going to watch the rest of the LPI highlights on TV. I'm fine."

"I won't be long, and I'll get us some lunch."

"Make sure it includes chips!" Keith shouted as Lucy left.

Lucy drove into town and found her favorite parking spot on her preferred parking level adjacent to the mall. As she exited the car and shut the door she noticed a shadow on the hood of the trunk. She looked, but no one was there.

Silly me, she said to herself. *I can't stop thinking that he's still following me.*

The doors to the mall were being held open by chains attached to the walls; the mall was always busy on Saturdays.

As she past the jewelry store, she noticed her reflection in the display window. She looked again. This time she felt nervous. It was the same shadow she saw on the trunk of her car. She missed a breath.

"It's okay," Lucy mumbled to herself.

She peered back into the reflection, wanting to make sure it wasn't her mind playing tricks again.

"May I help you?"

Lucy jumped. *Stupid me. Just the sales lady.*

"Just looking," Lucy replied as she reached into her bag for her phone.

Keith didn't answer. *The TV must be up too loud,* she thought to herself. She looked again at the window display and moved her head left to right, watching as the intense display lighting made the gold sparkle.

Lucy was suddenly forced against the glass, the energy from within the window drawing her closer. It was him again, drawing her into his personal space whenever she was alone.

"Lucy?"

No, go away.

"Come here, my sweet. I've been waiting for you all my life."

She looked at the floor under the display window, and it seemed to be cleaving. She knew the dark hole was dangerous, but she was drawn to this area. An escalator appeared. She knew that it would take her down under the shop. It started to move. She remembered being scared of escalators as a child and wondered why she wasn't scared now.

What will happen if I get on? she thought to herself. *Will I be ok? Why am I drawn to what lies beneath?*

The thought that there could be more gold below the shop weakened her. She lunged at the display. Passersby were watching. They came closer, but Lucy didn't notice the small crowd developing. The security cameras were stationary, focused on her. Lucy lunged again, smashing her face into the glass. A trickle of blood appeared under her nose. She stepped onto the escalator. Arms tried to grab her but it was too late. Lucy was on her way down.

To be continued …

"GOING DOWN" - PART 2

It's dark in here. Lucy's ride hit the concrete floor. *Where are the lights?* she wondered.

Her breath filled the dark air. It smelled musky. She put her arms out and did a 180° turn to feel for anything. She couldn't move; it was pitch black. She felt for the zipper on her bag. If she could get her phone out, it would give some light. She reached in, pulled it out, and pressed the buttons to reactivate it. Nothing. Keith had forgotten to put it on charger the night before, and now it was dead.

What next? I can't believe this is happening to me. Lucy moved her feet around in a 180° motion; she knew she had room to squat. *Well that's one positive thing*, she thought to herself.

Silence was deadly.

She tried to imagine what would be kept in storage under a jewelry shop. Would there be boxes in front or to the side of her? Was it worth the move off the elevator? What if it was summoned back up to the shop floor?

So many decisions—she just didn't know what to do. Time was passing by; surely someone would come soon.

There was a shuffling sound coming from behind the area to her left. "Hello?" Lucy said. "Is there anybody there?"

Rats? Oh my god! The thought of rats crossing over her feet sent cold shivers down her spine.

She sat and moved forward onto her hands and a knee, thinking this was the best option, a way forward and the least likely way to possibly injure herself.

She put her hand out and nervously put it onto the cold concrete floor. *Oh, I hope I don't put my knee on something furry.*

Lucy was making progress—three body movements forward and no accidents so far. The rustle came again. She stopped in her spot. "Hello?" she said again. But this time the rustle had a sniffle attached to it.

"Is anybody here? Hello?" She continued moving left.

Her hand reached out and touched what she believed was a hand. Jumping backwards, her heart racing, she tried to scramble back to the elevator, but it was nowhere to be found.

The rustling was getting closer. Lucy held her breath and her brow began to sweat in anticipation of her future.

"Hello, hello. Is it you? Are you there? Please let me know you are here!" Lucy, over the years, had become accustomed to the man showing up anywhere.

"Is it you? Are you down here with me?"

"Lucy, Lucy, Lucy," he repeated softly. "You are my obsession, my lovely lady. Possessed by each other, you are finally with me."

"This time you're mine and only mine. You weren't careful enough. You must be careful. I told you, Lucy, to be careful what you wish for."

Lucy's heart was racing. Her mind had totally gone blank. "Man, what is it that you want? You can't only want me!"

"Over the years, girl, you have run and tried to hide from me. I have watched you over and over again. Now, come closer. I want to run my fingers all over you."

"If I kiss you will you let me go?"

"No, Lucy. You tried that on me last time and you deceived me. I'm not going to let you do that again!" he screamed, close to her face.

"Now sit. Mmm, my love, you smell nice."

"Please don't hurt me. I like the feeling of being beside you. We should stay this way, just for a little while. They are going to get you this time."

"No, Lucy, they aren't, and if you are true to yourself, you will also know they won't. No one believes you, Lucy. You have tried so hard with your mother over the years. She knows who I am."

"You must go down now, Lucy. Sit still. That's my girl. I want to enjoy this moment I've waited a lifetime for!"

"You're a sick man."

"No, Lucy, the truth is you're my chosen one. Move closer."

Lucy resisted with all her power not to move closer. The man smelled rancid, the same as he did years ago. The thought of him touching her hair was enough to make her cry.

"Don't cry, Lucy. It's alright. I've loved you too much. Now you are my only possession."

He scratched her neck with his broken nails. A trickle of blood ran down Lucy's neck and she felt it seep into her white blouse.

His hands reached into her blouse. She slapped her hands towards that area and turned to cover herself, trembling on the spot.

"What is wrong with you, Lucy?"

"Don't touch me. You're revolting!"

"No, Lucy, you mustn't say that now. You and I are together forever. We will live off each other. When you're in love, you don't need food or water. We can survive on love alone."

Lucy desperately reached into her handbag. She shuffled around, searching for the bottle. She found it. This was her last chance. She twisted off the top and swallowed three tablets. She waited. Her mother was right; it was true for all these years. He was the shadow of her mind.

Ends

"WIRED BLOOD"

I pass onto and into the night, my feelings of fright following me. When will they end? *Why* won't they end? Shadows are creeping up on me. I can't stand the pain.

The days come to light, but my world is still full of darkness. Roy, Keith, whoever you are—are you both real or are you just thoughts and objects in my imagination? Who actually did come first? Was it you, Keith, or was it you, Roy?

Now, stop! Stop right there, thank you very much. I don't need my palms laced with silver powder anymore, Miss. Is it you who brings me down into this world of confusion, wiring my blood with that paste of yours?

I want a normal life, please. Please, I've had enough. Listen to me.

Is there anybody out there who feels the same pain?

Stop! No! Get away from me. Don't dare come any closer! I'm in charge of my own destiny now. I've made a decision. This decision is to *stop*.

No tablets or paste ever again. The signals will now be allowed to run free in my brain. These currents will control me but, this time, the right way.

It now must end. I know the end is near. Near to me. There is no other horizon in sight; this blood of mine is boiling out of sight.

Didn't you hear me, Miss? No more paste! I'm normal now. I don't need *you;* I don't need *anybody* else to be with me.

I'm normal, Miss. Can't you see?

My words are straightforward; my blood pressure is fine. No more drugs for me.

Mum said she would come soon. I promised her that I would do fine. My chart says I'm fine. What's this? What does it say here? I'm *not* normal? How dare they say that! Maybe that was yesterday but not today. I feel fine.

I'm not weird. Who gives you the right to criticize me?

I'm just bored with my life. There's no excitement, no light.

It's an ordeal to make it through the night. Don't you care? Don't you understand?

Where is my sunshine? Where is my wine? Don't you worry your pretty little heads. I'm not going to hit the bottle and re-drink the red.

Lock me up? How dare you chase me again? Go away, man. Go away. You're no help in my new life.

That's the problem, man—*you.* They say that to me over and over again, all the time, in fact.

If you just go away and hide they said they'll let me out of here. Once I'm free, I'll let you know, and then you can come back—when we are free.

No one will know; it'll be our secret. You love secrets; you told me that all my life.

The doctor said that what I focus on is what I feel. So I will no longer focus on you so I won't feel you. That's why the doctors wire my blood with that sticky paste, to slow down the thoughts of you, now and forever. You will become my past.

I know we said we loved each other. I know it's true that we did. Yes, we spent many hours together, but all I know is that we must now part.

I will love you forever and ever because you have loved me unconditionally. You are very powerful and will remain always in my heart.

Man, this is the time we must part. These wires are coming out of my heart. It will be the end of us, I know, but it must happen.

I will be back, and I know you will be back, but for now we must separate and move forward to gain momentum as we move in separate ways.

We will be free; just wait and you will feel it. You will be single and I will be single, and our lives will be like before we met.

It's the end now. Goodbye. Our molds have been broken. I'm feeling normal again. The sun is shining and life is beautiful.

I will always love you.

"Man, you mustn't call me again," I whispered as I walked past the hospital admissions desk for the last time, "I won't be around."

Ends

Lightning Source UK Ltd.
Milton Keynes UK
23 December 2010

164768UK00010B/1/P